Hide

and Squeak

Heather Vogel Frederick

Illustrated by C. F. Payne

Simon & Schuster Books for Young Readers
NEW YORK   LONDON   TORONTO   SYDNEY

Mouse baby, mouse baby,
where can you be?
I can't see you. Can you see me?
It's time for bed. It's time for sleep.
No more time for hide-and-squeak.

Wiggle a whisker.

Wiggle a tail.

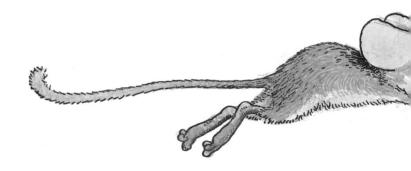

Mouse baby dashes off . . .

but Daddy's on his trail.

Chase him round the garden.

Chase him to the house.

Chase him through the back door.

What a speedy little mouse!

Mouse baby, mouse baby,

where can you be?

I can't see you.

Can you see me?

It's time for bed. It's time for sleep.

No more time for hide-and-squeak.

Wiggle a whisker. Wiggle a tail.

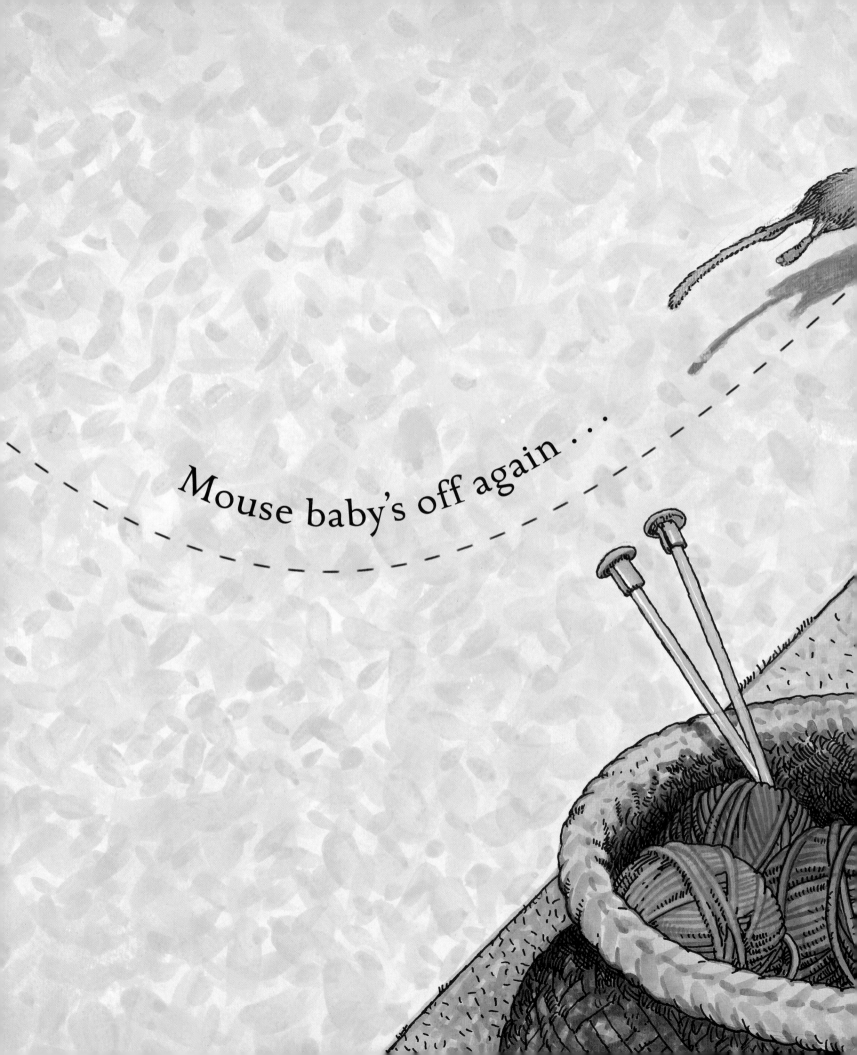

Mouse baby's off again . . .

but Daddy's on his trail.

Chase him past the sofa.

Chase him round the lamp.

Chase him up the curtains.

What a plucky little scamp!

Mouse baby, mouse baby,
are you by the clock?
The one atop the mantel with the loud

TICK-TOCK?

It's time for bed. It's time for sleep.
No more time for hide-and-squeak.

Scurry up the staircase.
Scamper down the hall.
Splash into the bathtub
with a giant cannonball!

Mouse baby, mouse baby,
where can you be?
I can't see you. Can you see me?

Look, beneath the soapsuds!
Look, beneath the cloth!
There's my little rascal,
hiding in the froth.

Daddy sees your whiskers!

Daddy's on your trail!

Daddy catches Baby
by his mouse baby tail . . .

swings him high for a kiss,

swings him low for a hug,

then tucks him under covers,
like a bug in a rug.

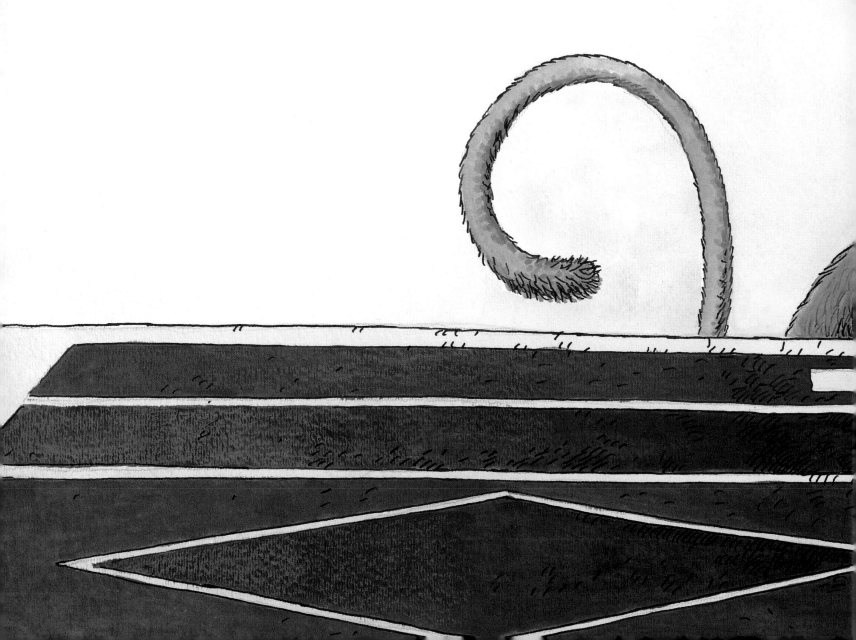

It's time for bed.
It's time for sleep.
It's time for an end
to hide-and-squeak.

For Steve, who wrangled our two little squeakers with such glee
—H. V. F.

I dedicate the art in this book to my family
for their love that carries me through
—C. F. P.

SIMON & SCHUSTER BOOKS FOR YOUNG READERS • An imprint of Simon & Schuster Children's Publishing Division • 1230 Avenue of the Americas, New York, New York 10020 • Text copyright © 2011 by Heather Vogel Frederick • Illustrations copyright © 2011 by C. F. Payne All rights reserved, including the right of reproduction in whole or in part in any form. SIMON & SCHUSTER BOOKS FOR YOUNG READERS is a trademark of Simon & Schuster, Inc. • For information about special discounts for bulk purchases, please contact Simon & Schuster Special Sales at 1-866-506-1949 or business@simonandschuster.com. The Simon & Schuster Speakers Bureau can bring authors to your live event. For more information or to book an event, contact the Simon & Schuster Speakers Bureau at 1-866-248-3049 or visit our website at www.simonspeakers.com. • Book design by Chloë Foglia • The text for this book is set in Golden Cockerel. • The illustrations for this book are rendered in a mixture of pen and ink, acrylics, and colored pencils on watercolor paper. • Manufactured in China • 0710 SCP • 10 9 8 7 6 5 4 3 2 1 • Library of Congress Cataloging-in-Publication Data • Frederick, Heather Vogel. • Hide-and-squeak / Heather Vogel Frederick ; illustrated by C. F. Payne. • p. cm. • Summary: A mouse baby leads his father on a merry game of hide-and-squeak at bedtime. • ISBN 978-0-689-85570-2 (hardcover) • [1. Stories in rhyme. 2. Bedtime—Fiction. 3. Father and child—Fiction. 4. Mice—Fiction.] I. Payne, C. F., ill. II. Title. • PZ8.3.F869Hi 2010 • [E]—dc22 • 2008039648